# My "x, y, z" Sound Box®

**Library of Congress Cataloging-in-Publication Data**
Moncure, Jane Belk.
My "x, y, z" sound box / by Jane Belk Moncure; illustrated by Colin King.
p. cm.
Summary: Three characters find words beginning with the letter "x," "y," and "z"
to put in their sound boxes
ISBN 1-56766-790-2 (lib. reinforced : alk. paper)
[1. Alphabet.] I. King, Colin, ill.  II. Title.
PZ7.M739 Myx   2000
[E]—dc21                99-056563

# My "x,y,z"
## Sound Box®

Jane Belk Moncure

*illustrated by* Colin King

The Child's World®

Little  **X** had a box.

"I will find things that begin
with my letter," he said.

"I will put them into my sound  box."

Little  found an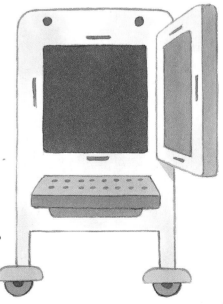

x-ray machine.

"Excellent," said Little  .

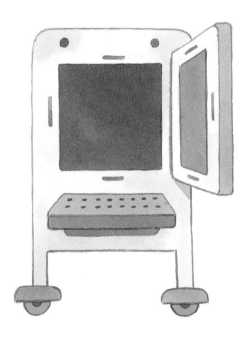

"With my x-ray machine,
I can see inside things."

"I will take an x-ray of my hands."

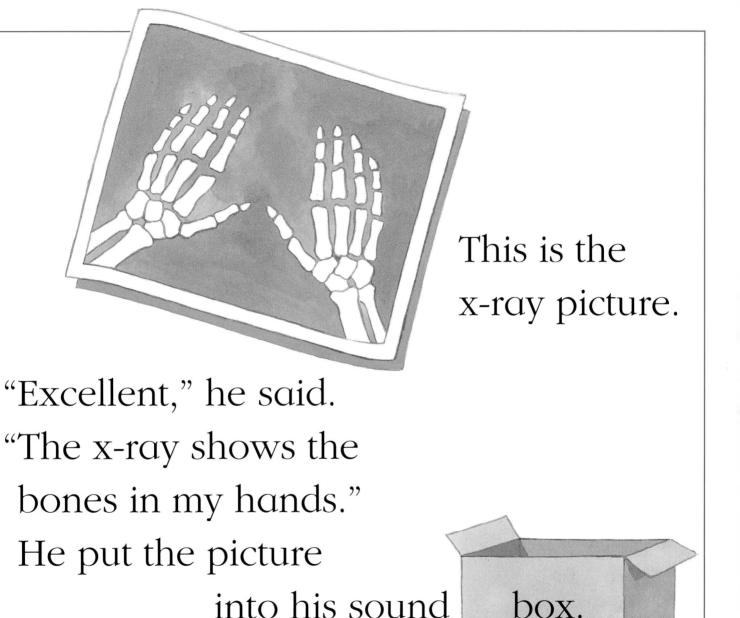

This is the
x-ray picture.

"Excellent," he said.
"The x-ray shows the
bones in my hands."
He put the picture
into his sound box.

"I will take an
x-ray of my feet,"
he said.

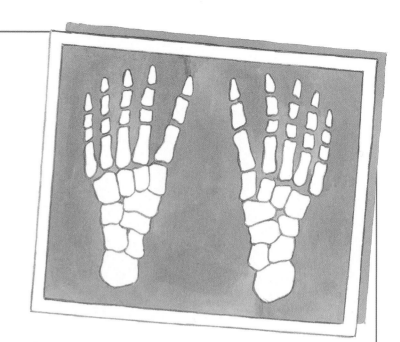

This is the x-ray picture.

"Excellent," said Little
"The x-ray shows the
bones in my feet."

Then he put the x-ray picture
and the x-ray machine

into his sound          box.

He said, "Now I will call my friend . . .

Little  y.

I will see if he has a box."

"I do," said Little 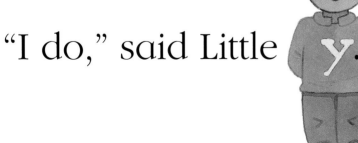 y.

"I will find something that begins with my 'y' sound.

I will put it into my sound box."

Little y found a yo-yo.

It was a yellow yo-yo.

He tried to make the yo-yo go

down . . . and . . . up.

But the string was too short.

Little **y** found some yarn.

He tied it to the string.

Little  and see if she has

a    box."

"I do," said Little Z.

"I will find things that begin with my 'z' sound.

I will put them into my sound box."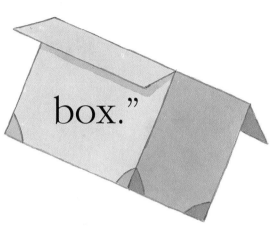

She found a zebra . . .

and another zebra,

and another zebra.

Little  caught the three

zebras

and . . .

tried to put them into the box.

# But the zebras jumped out of the box!

Zip!

Zip!

Zip!

They ran

zigzag down the road.

"I will catch you, zippy zebras!"
called Little Z.

And she did.

Then she took the
zebras to the zoo.

More about Little 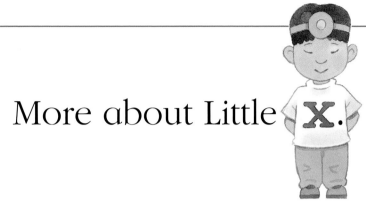 **X**.

In our story, we just used the letter "x" in front of the word "ray," making "x-ray." But in other words, Little x has the "z" sound. Can you read these words with the "z" sound?

xylophone

Xerox machine

Xerox is a brand name for a kind of copying machine.

# Can you read these words with Little  ?

yams

yacht

yard

yak

Can you read these words with Little 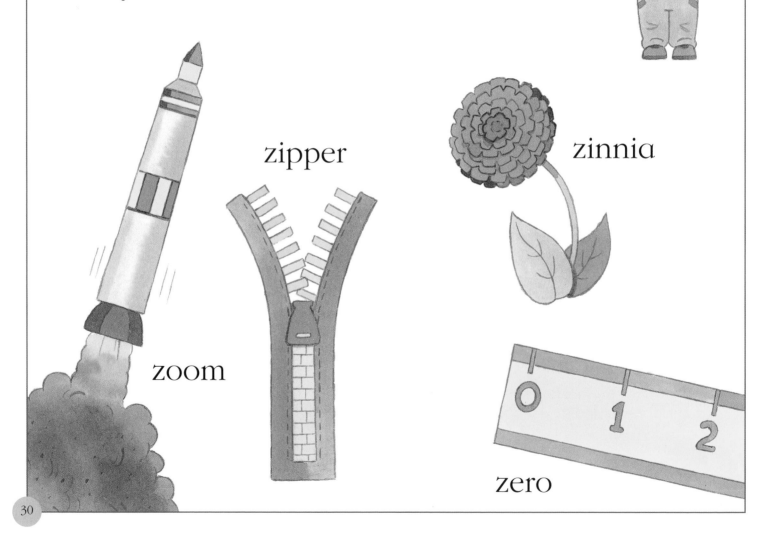?

zipper

zinnia

zoom

zero

## ABOUT THE AUTHOR AND ILLUSTRATOR

**Jane Belk Moncure** began her writing career when she was in kindergarten. She has never stopped writing. Many of her children's stories and poems have been published, to the delight of young readers, including her son Jim, whose childhood experiences found their way into many of her books.

Mrs. Moncure's writing is based upon an active career in early childhood education. A recipient of an M.A. degree from Columbia University, Mrs. Moncure has taught and directed nursery, kindergarten, and primary grade programs in California, New York, Virginia, and North Carolina. As a former member of the faculties of Virginia Commonwealth University and the University of Richmond, she taught prospective teachers in early childhood education.

Mrs. Moncure has travelled extensively abroad, studying early childhood programs in the United Kingdom, The Netherlands, and Switzerland. She was the first president of the Virginia Association for Early Childhood Education and received its award for outstanding service to young children.

A resident of North Carolina, Mrs. Moncure is currently a full-time writer and educational consultant. She is married to Dr. James A. Moncure, former vice president of Elon College.

**Colin King** studied at the Royal College of Art, London. He started his freelance career as an illustrator, working for magazines and advertising agencies.

He began drawing pictures for children's books in 1976 and has illustrated over sixty titles to date.

Included in a wide variety of subjects are a best-selling children's encyclopedia and books about spies and detectives.

His books have been translated into several languages, including Japanese and Hebrew. He has four grown-up children and lives in Suffolk, England, with his wife, three dogs, and a cat.